Snake

BY
CAROLINE ARNOLD
PHOTOGRAPHS BY
RICHARD HEWETT

MORROW JUNIOR BOOKS
NEW YORK

Title page photo: rosy boa.
Acknowledgment page photo: vine snake.

PHOTO CREDITS: Permission to use the following photograph is gratefully acknowledged: Robert Applegate, page 34 (both).

The text type is 14 point Meridien.

Library of Congress Cataloging-in-Publication Data. Arnold, Caroline. Snake / by Caroline Arnold ; photographs by Richard Hewett.   p.   cm. Includes index. Summary: Describes the physical characteristics, behavior, and life cycle of several kinds of snakes, especially the boas and pythons. ISBN 0-688-09409-0 (trade).—ISBN 0-688-09410-4 (library) 1. Snakes—Juvenile literature.   [1. Snakes.]   I. Hewett, Richard.   II. Title. QL666.06A76 1991 597.96—dc20 90-22591 CIP AC

Acknowledgments

We are extremely grateful to the Los Angeles Zoo, both for reviewing the text and for providing us with the opportunity to learn about and photograph their snakes. In particular, we thank Harvey M. Fischer, Curator of Reptiles; June Bottcher, Special Programs Assistant; and Jay Kilgore, owner of Baby. We also thank zoo staff Katherine Nevins, Rose-Marie Weisz, Sara Canchola, Tad Motoyama, Jeff Briscoe, and Dennis Thurslond, as well as Sasha Sircus, Matthew Felman, Tiffany Tropp, and Jennifer Arnold for their enthusiastic participation in the photographs. We thank Robert Applegate, Robert Kenyon, Judy Ludlam, and Dana Bleitz for their cheerful assistance, too. And, as always, we are most appreciative of the support of our editor, Andrea Curley.

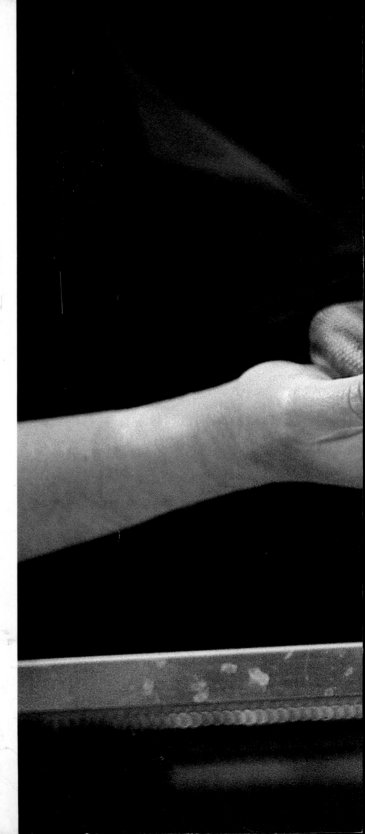

Rosy boa.

Rosy lifted her head when she felt the vibration of her cage top being removed. Then, as a warm hand gently picked her up, Rosy curled her long, scaly body around it to get a better grip while being raised into the air. Rapidly flicking her slender tongue, she stretched forward and began to investigate her new surroundings.

Rosy, a North American snake called the rosy boa, is used in one of the educational programs of the Los Angeles Zoo. Because she is accustomed to being handled, volunteer staff from the zoo take Rosy to schools, hospitals, and community centers so that people can see her up close and learn more about these limbless reptiles. Most people do not have a chance to see snakes very often and are afraid of them. Some snakes are dangerous and must be treated with extreme caution, but most snakes, such as the rosy boa, are not harmful as long as they are handled carefully.

Different types of boas as well as many other kinds of snakes live in the reptile house at the Los Angeles Zoo. Some of them are kept in glass-walled terrariums; others live in exhibits where visitors can view them through large windows. Each enclosure is made to be as much like the snake's natural habitat as possible. Some have sand or leaf mold on the bottom, some have branches for climbing, and others have rocks and leaves for hiding places. A door at the back of each enclosure allows zoo keepers to give the snakes food and water and to clean the displays.

Emerald tree boa (right).

Snakes belong to a large class of animals called reptiles. Other reptile groups include lizards, crocodiles, turtles, a lizardlike animal called the tuatara, and the now extinct dinosaurs. Most reptile bodies are covered with tough scales made of a thickened form of skin containing keratin. (This substance is also found in fingernails, claws, and a rattlesnake's rattle.) The shape and size of the scales vary depending on where they are located on the snake's body. They also differ from species to species. For instance, the bodies of boas and pythons have many rows of small, smooth scales, whereas rattlesnakes have larger, coarser scales in fewer rows. Many people think that the scales of reptiles are slimy, but if you touch a snake, you will find that its skin is smooth and dry.

A snake may also feel cool to the touch. Like fish and amphibians, reptiles are cold-blooded animals. Their body temperature changes with the temperature of the air around them. That is why, in the wild, you may see a snake or lizard warming itself in the sun on a cool day. Warm-blooded animals such as birds and mammals are able to maintain a constant body temperature. For instance, your temperature stays at about 98.6 degrees Fahrenheit (37 degrees Celsius) unless you are sick and have a fever.

Reptiles need to be warm to move, although, like almost all animals, they cannot live long at temperatures of more than 100 degrees Fahrenheit (38 degrees Celsius). Snakes that live in the desert go underground or seek shade during the heat of the day. Snakes that live in the jungle may go into water or under damp vegetation when it is hot.

In cold weather, a reptile is sluggish. It cannot feed, and because it moves slowly, it is more likely to be caught by predators. Snakes that live in climates with freezing winters usually hibernate, or become inactive, during those months. The temperature at the zoo's reptile house is kept at about 80 to 85 degrees Fahrenheit (27 to 29 degrees Celsius) year round so the animals do not get either too hot or too cold.

Snakes live in most parts of the world except in New Zealand and Ireland, some other islands, and in places where the ground is permanently frozen. The greatest variety of snakes live in places where the climate is warm year round.

In the wild, the rosy boa is found in the deserts and rocky foothills of Southern California, Arizona, Mexico, and Baja California. Because the days are often hot there, the rosy boa is active mainly at night, when the air is cooler. Although chiefly a ground dweller, it sometimes climbs low bushes looking for prey.

The rosy boa is a medium-sized snake with a small head and a blunt tail. They can grow to 42 inches (107.7 centimeters) in length and have smooth, stout bodies covered with 35 to 45 rows of tiny, iridescent scales.

Desert rosy boa.

As in most other species of snakes, male and female rosy boas look nearly alike. However, if a male and female of about the same size were placed next to each other, the male would have a slightly shorter body and a longer, broader-based tail. The tail is the portion beyond the opening, or *vent,* on the underside of the snake. A snake gets rid of body wastes at the vent. Reproductive organs are also located there.

The scientific name of the rosy boa, *Lichanura trivirgata,* refers to the three stripes along the length of the body. Among the three subspecies of rosy boas, there are slight differences in the color of these stripes. The Mexican rosy boa has distinct brown stripes and black speckles on its belly; the desert rosy boa has rose-colored or light brown stripes and brown belly speckles; and the coastal rosy boa has less clearly marked pink or light brown stripes. Although each subspecies is found in a different location, all three have similar habits and behavior. Rosy is a desert rosy boa.

Red-tailed boa constrictor.

The rosy boa belongs to a group of snakes with the scientific name Boidae. Most members of the boid family, which includes all the boas and pythons, have large, powerful jaws; long teeth; and long, muscular bodies. Only one species of boa is actually called the boa constrictor, although all of the boids use their bodies to squeeze, or constrict, their prey.

Boas live in North and South America and are found from southern Canada to Argentina. The rosy boa and the rubber boa are the only species found in the United States. While both the rosy boa and the rubber boa are relatively small snakes, others, such as the boa constrictor, grow to 18 feet (5.5 meters) and are among the largest snakes in the world.

The size and body shape of each species of snake vary according to where it lives and how it behaves. The emerald tree boa on page 9, for example, spends most of its life in the jungle treetops, where it catches birds to eat. Its long, thin shape is well suited to climbing and wrapping around branches. The anaconda, on the other hand, lives on the jungle floor and has a thick, heavy body. It is the largest species of snake alive, and its members have been known to grow to 37½ feet (11.4 meters) in length. The anaconda spends much of its time in the water and, like most snakes, is a good swimmer. Because its eyes are on top of its head, the anaconda can see even when partly submerged.

In the zoo, a heat lamp helps keep the anaconda warm.

Baby, an Indian python.

Pythons differ from boas in having an extra bone in the skull that creates a slightly higher ridge above the eyes. Also, pythons reproduce by laying eggs, whereas boas give birth to live young. Pythons are found in Southeast Asia, the East Indies, Africa, and Australia. The ball python, a medium-sized snake, gets its name from the way it rolls itself into a ball to hide from predators. Until recently, the reticulated python of Southeast Asia, which can grow to 33 feet (10 meters) in length, was considered the longest snake in the world. The discovery of a longer anaconda makes the re-

ticulated python the second-largest snake.

The Los Angeles Zoo is home to an Indian python named Baby. Baby belongs to one of the keepers, who has loaned her to the zoo. The keeper raised Baby from the time she was hatched and named her when she was small. At birth, Baby was about 2 feet (.6 meter) long and weighed about 4 ounces (114.3 grams). Now, at the age of six, Baby measures 15 feet (4.6 meters) in length and weighs 160 pounds (72.7 kilograms). She is expected to live about twenty years and will continue to grow all her life.

Ball python.

Because a snake has no limbs and often has no clearly defined neck, it seems to be an animal made of only a head and a tail. However, like other animals with backbones, it has a heart, lungs, and other vital organs located along its body.

The long body of a snake bends easily and can slip through narrow openings. This makes it ideal for moving through grass or dense jungle vegetation, into small holes, or between rocks. Legs are not necessary for moving through this kind of environment and can even get in the way.

Although the first snakes, which lived more than 100 million years ago, probably had short limbs like those of lizards, these legs gradually disappeared as their bodies adapted to a new way of life.

One of the amazing features of boas and pythons is the tiny rear leg bones that they still have near the tail. At the end of each leg is a small claw called a *spur*. Although the leg bones are hidden inside the snake's body, you can see the spurs where they emerge on the underside of a boa or python at its vent. The spurs of the male are longer than those of the female and are used to stroke the female during courtship.

Spurs on the underside of D'Albert's python.

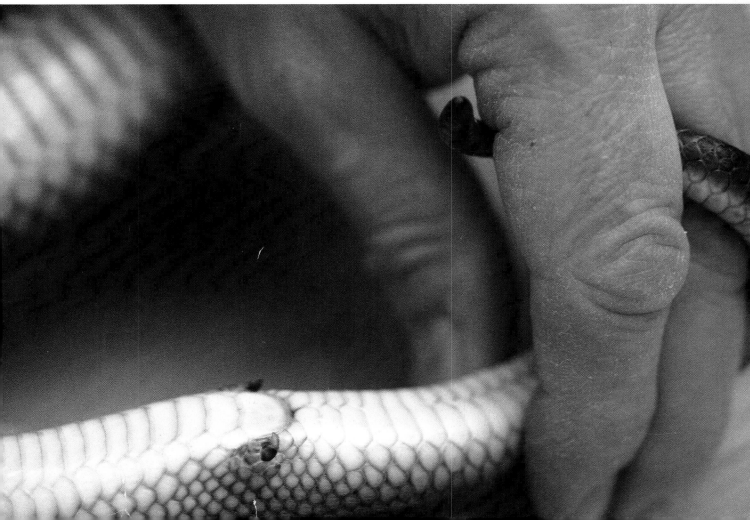

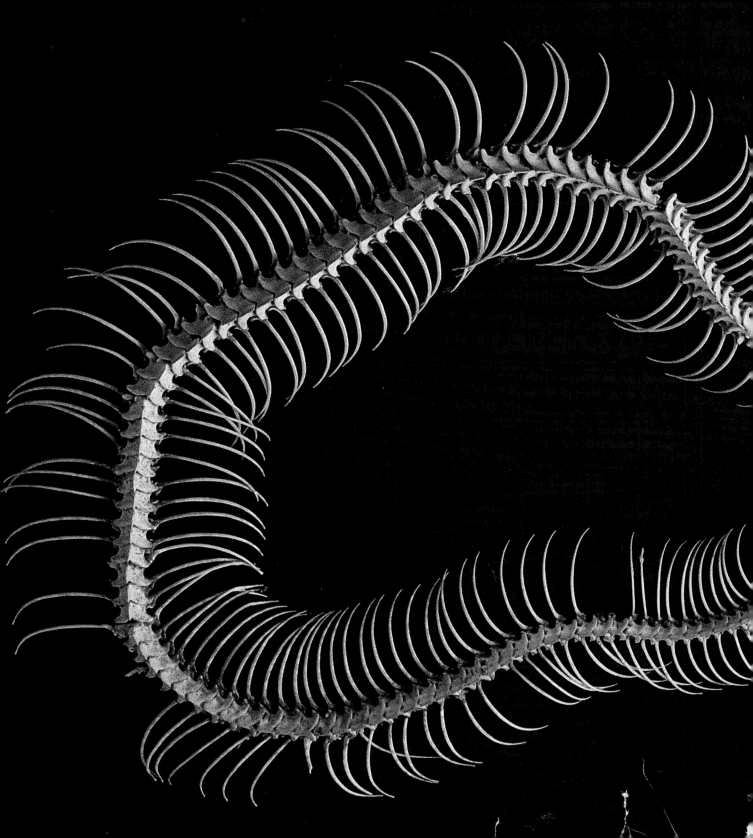

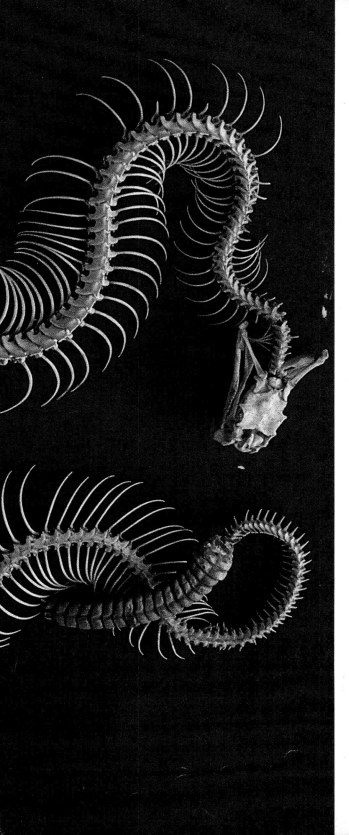

Skeleton of a western rattlesnake.

As in other animals with backbones, the body of a snake is supported by a series of small bones in the back called *vertebrae*. You can feel the lumps of your vertebrae by rubbing your hand along your spine. Except at the neck and tail, each of the snake's vertebrae is connected to a pair of ribs that circle around the inner body organs. People usually have only twelve pairs of ribs; a snake has dozens. Some very flexible snakes have more than 400 pairs of ribs!

The forward motion of a rosy boa forms an S.

Snakes move in a variety of ways. On open ground, the body usually bends to form an *S* shape. As the head moves forward, the muscles of the snake's body expand and contract so that the body follows in a wavy path. The same motion is used when a snake swims. Although cartoons often show snakes moving in an up-and-down zigzag pattern, they never do this. The curves of the snake's body are almost always flat to the surface on which it is moving.

When climbing a thin tree, a snake grips the trunk tightly with the muscles in the tail end of its body and then, in the same way that a gymnast climbs a rope, stretches its body upward. After each upward push, the snake grips the tree with the upper part of its body and lifts its tail to a higher position; then it pushes again. When climbing a tree with rough bark, the snake can grip the ridges in the bark with its muscles and move up and around the tree in the same

way that it would move across the ground.

The sidewinder snake has a unique motion that allows it to move quickly across the shifting sands of the desert where it lives. It lifts its body in sections and pushes in a sideways motion.

In most snakes, each pair of ribs is attached to a large scale on the underside of its body called a *scute*. The scutes overlap, with the thin edge pointing toward the back of the snake. As the muscles attached to each rib pull part of the body forward, the scutes catch on to the surface of the ground like tractor treads. When a snake uses this technique to move forward in a straight line, this motion appears as a ripple moving along the snake's body. Boas, pythons, and rattlesnakes often move in this way. A snake cannot move well over a slippery surface because the scutes have nothing to grip.

Russell's viper.

Although snakes can move quickly when necessary, they spend most of their time resting quietly. A motionless snake is often difficult to see because its coloring may blend into that of its background. For instance, the dark and light patches of the Russell's viper look like the dappled shade of the forest floor. The mottled coloring of many rattlesnakes is similar to that of the sand and rocks in the areas where they live. At first glance, the tree-dwelling vine snake appears to be just another jungle branch.

Protective coloring helps a snake hide from its enemies, which include birds, lizards, some mammals, and even other snakes. The earth tones of the rosy boa make it hard for large birds such as hawks, eagles, or the speedy roadrunner to see it in the shadows of the rock crevices where the snake is often found.

Usually, a snake prefers to escape from its enemy rather than to confront it. If it is cornered, however, the snake will defend itself or try to scare the predator away. Many snakes indicate that they are annoyed by hissing. To hiss, a snake forcefully expels air from its lungs. Some species of snakes have other specialized methods of warning, such as giving off unpleasant odors or, in the case of rattlesnakes, making noises with their tails. Snakes often bite if they are provoked, and even if the bite is not venomous, it can hurt.

Vine snake.

Green tree python.

Camouflage also helps a snake conceal itself while hunting or waiting for prey. All snakes are carnivorous, that is, meat eaters. Their food varies depending on the species and includes tiny insects, fish, grubs, worms, eggs, birds, lizards, other snakes, and small mammals. Just like other animals, a snake relies on its senses to locate and capture prey, to find its way around its environment, and to protect itself.

Most snakes have fairly good eyesight and, because they have no eyelids, appear to be constantly on the alert. Their eyes are open all the time, even when they are sleeping. The pupil of the eye opens and closes like a camera lens to let in varying amounts of light. The pupils of night-hunting snakes, such as the rosy boa, usually appear as slits during the day, whereas the eyes of day hunters are fully open. Often it is hard to see a snake's eyes because the color matches that of the surrounding scales. A hard transparent covering, called a *spectacle,* protects each of the snake's eyes.

Indian python; the forked tongue helps detect odors.

One of the most important senses for a snake is that of smell. Watch a snake explore its surroundings. Its forked tongue constantly darts in and out of its mouth. A small triangular hole at the front of the snake's mouth allows the tongue to go in and out, even when the mouth is closed. The tongue picks up tiny scent molecules from the air and brings them inside the mouth to a highly sensitive organ of taste and smell called the *Jacobson's organ*. Smells coming in as the snake breathes also pass by the Jacobson's organ.

Usually, a snake breathes through the nostrils on its snout. However, when it eats, these holes may be blocked by food. Then the snake can push its windpipe forward along the floor of its mouth and breathe directly through it.

A python has two rows of sharp teeth.

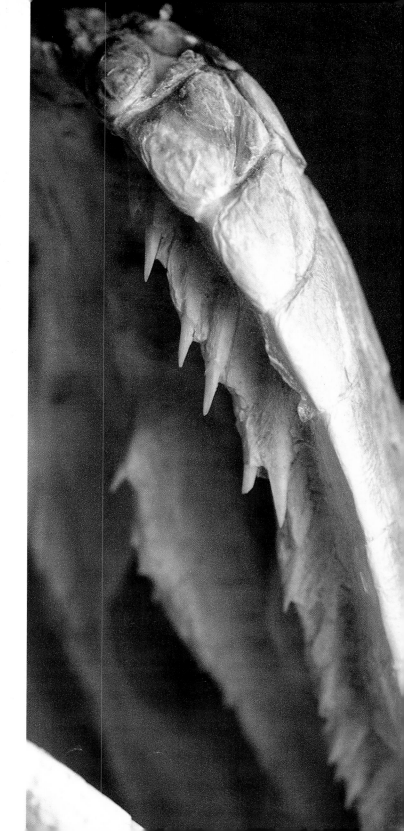

Like that of other snakes, Rosy's head has no outer ears or earholes. Although a snake may be able to hear some airborne noises, it hears chiefly by sensing vibrations in the ground. These vibrations pass through the snake's body to ear bones inside the skull and allow the snake to sense an approaching animal even before it comes into view. If the vibrations indicate that the animal is large, the snake has time to hide or escape. If the vibrations are small, the snake may wait until the animal goes by and try to catch it.

Each side of a snake's mouth is lined with long rows of sharp teeth, which are used to grip its food and prevent it from escaping. The teeth point toward the throat and thus keep food from slipping backward out of the mouth.

Although wild rosy boas sometimes eat small lizards and birds, their main prey is small rodents. At the zoo, most of the snakes of Rosy's size are given mice to eat. As soon as Rosy senses that a mouse has been put in her enclosure, she strikes it with open jaws and grabs it in her mouth. Then, even though the keeper has already killed the mouse to prevent it from harming Rosy, the snake quickly coils herself around the mouse's body just as she would if it were alive. For several minutes she squeezes the mouse so tightly that if it had been breathing, it would no longer be able to do so and would die.

A snake cannot use its slender teeth to chew or cut up its food. Instead, it swallows the food whole, usually starting with the head. First the snake stretches its mouth around the head of its prey. (Unlike the jaws of most other animals, the two halves of a snake's jaw are not fastened solidly together at the back. Therefore, they can separate and enlarge the opening between them.) At the same time, the skin around the snake's head and neck stretches like a sheet of elastic. In this way the snake can swallow food that is larger than its own body diameter.

The snake uses its teeth to draw the food into its mouth. First one jaw slides forward and pulls the prey; then the other jaw does the same. Little by little, the food is pulled in and swallowed. Saliva helps the food slip easily from the mouth into the throat. Then, in the stomach, powerful juices digest the food. These liquids are so strong that they can even dissolve small bones. Complete digestion may take several days or longer. The only parts of its prey that a snake cannot digest are teeth, hair, and feathers. These are passed out from the body at the vent along with other waste products.

Male (left) and female (right) rosy boas.

After it has eaten, a snake may not be hungry again for a week or two or even longer, depending on how active it is and the size of the previous meal. Usually, Rosy is fed a mouse every other week. During periods of inactivity, a snake may go for months without food.

In temperate climates like that of the United States, most snakes become inactive during the cooler winter months. They go underground or curl up in deep rock crevices until spring comes. Then, as the days lengthen and the air grows warmer, the snakes emerge to look for food and mates.

Most snakes are ready to breed in their third year. Boas and other snakes that produce live young are called *ovoviviparous*. Those that lay eggs are *oviparous*. A female snake with eggs or young inside her body is said to be *gravid*.

In the wild, rosy boas mate during May and June, after which males and females go their separate ways. About four months later, during October and

November, the female produces from six to ten baby snakes, each about 12 inches (30.8 centimeters) long. While it is developing inside the female, each baby snake is encased in a tough, transparent sac. This sac is not connected to the mother's body and is like the inside of an egg without a shell. When the baby snakes are developed, the female expels them through her vent. Each tiny snake breaks through its sac and emerges into the air. Then the mother snake slithers away, leaving the young snakes to fend for themselves. Young rosy boas feed on baby mice, small lizards, and other small animals.

Eight-week-old rosy boa.

Burmese python laying eggs.

Hatching albino prairie king snakes.

An oviparous female snake lays her eggs one to two months after mating. In some cases, a female stores the male's sperm in her body and can produce fertile eggs during the following year as well. When she is ready to lay her eggs, she looks for a protected spot, such as under the edge of a stone, among rotting leaves, or in an old stump. Depending on her size and species, a female snake will lay from 15 to 100 leathery-shelled, oval eggs. While the baby snakes are growing inside, the dampness of the earth keeps the eggs moist and soft, and the sun and rotting vegetation keep them slightly warm. People who raise snakes in captivity usually remove the eggs from the female snake's enclosure and place them in a container inside an incubator to prevent them from drying out and to keep them at the proper temperature.

In almost all species, the female snake leaves her eggs after they have been laid and does not return. Pythons are an exception to this rule. The female python lays her eggs in a compact pile and curls her body around them. By twitching her muscles, she is able to raise her body temperature several degrees above that of the surrounding air and keep the eggs warm.

Forty to seventy days after the egg was laid, a young snake is ready to hatch. It pushes upward on its shell, using a sharp projection in the front of its mouth to slice the shell open. This tiny projection, called the *egg tooth*, is lost shortly after hatching. Soon after the eggshell is opened, the young snake begins to breathe air. Then it slips out of the shell to the outside world.

From the moment of hatching, the young snakes, which look like tiny versions of their parents, are independent. Although they may stay for a short while in the area of the nest, they must soon be ready to find their own food and defend themselves.

A young snake grows rapidly, doubling its size within its first year. Throughout a snake's life, its outer layer of skin is regularly replaced with a new one. This is called *shedding*. Just before shedding, the old skin dries and loosens, causing the snake's color to appear dull. One sign that shedding will take place soon is that the spectacles over the eyes become cloudy or bluish.

Shedding often occurs at night, although it may happen anytime. The complete process usually takes several hours or more. The skin first detaches around the snout. Then, by rubbing against rocks, sand, or rough branches, the snake wiggles forward out of its skin, much as a person might pull off a tight-fitting glove. The skin folds backward as the snake moves forward and is thus turned inside out.

Young snakes may shed as often as every forty-five days during the warm months when they are active and eating a lot. Older snakes grow more slowly and shed less often. Snakes grow and shed throughout their lifetime, which may be twenty-five years or more. You can often find shed skins if you look outdoors in the summer in places where snakes live. The outline of each scale is visible in the papery skin, and if you look closely, you can see the spectacles, which resemble tiny contact lenses.

There are more than three thousand different species of snakes in the world. Scientists divide them into families according to body structure. Although there is some disagreement about the number of snake families, the usual number is eleven. In addition to the boid family, these are colubrids, two families of blind snakes, the sunbeam snake, pipe snakes, shieldtail snakes, pit vipers, vipers, elapids, and sea snakes.

About half of all the snakes in the world belong to the colubrid family. This group includes the common harmless snakes such as garter snakes, racers, king snakes, and bull snakes. Colubrids live all over the world and are the kind of snakes you are most likely to find near where you live.

There are two families of blind snakes, the typhlopids and leptotyphlopids. They are harmless and live chiefly in the tropics. This group includes the smallest snake in the world, which is only 4 inches (10.2 centimeters) long. Like other blind snakes, it has eyes, but they are undeveloped and hidden under scales.

The xenopeltid family has only one member, the sunbeam snake. This snake is 3 feet (.9 meter) long and has shiny scales. It is found in Southeast Asia.

Members of the aniliid family, or pipe snakes, are found in South America and Asia. These burrowing snakes get their name from their pipe-shaped bodies. Like boas and pythons in the boid family, they have the remnants of small hind limbs.

Another family of burrowing snakes is the brightly colored shieldtail snakes, called uropeltids. They are found in Sri Lanka and southern India. Their tails end in a distinctive flat disk. The sunbeam snake, pipe snakes, and shieldtail snakes are all harmless.

Some snakes are dangerous because they possess hollow fangs connected to special glands containing venom. Some species of colubrids have small fangs in the rear of the mouth, but in most cases their venom is weak and not dangerous to humans. The most dangerous snakes inject venom into their prey through sharp fangs in the front of the mouth. Some of their venom is so powerful it can kill a person.

Snake venom is of two types. Neurotoxins are venoms that affect the nervous system and are the most dangerous. As they spread through the body in the bloodstream, they paralyze muscles until the heart or lungs stop working. Hemotoxins break down blood cells. Blood transports oxygen to body cells. Without oxygen, the cells cannot live. A snake can produce one or both types of venom. Normally, snakes use their venom to immobilize prey before eating it. Most snakes bite people or large animals only when threatened or startled.

It is important to learn to recognize the venomous snakes that live in your area. If you go hiking in places where venomous snakes live, look ahead on the trail and avoid reaching up onto ledges where a snake might possibly be lying.

Large fangs are located at the front of this western rattlesnake skull.

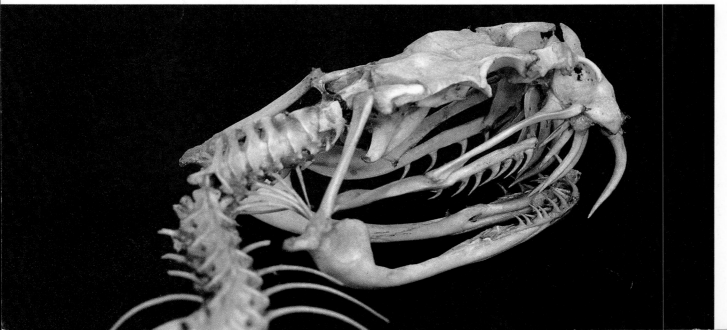

Neotropical rattlesnake.

The crotalids, or pit vipers, are a family of venomous snakes found in many parts of North America, South America, and Asia. Pit vipers get their name from cavities, called *loreal pits,* on the front of their snouts, behind the nostrils. These pits are heat sensors and allow the snake to locate a warm-blooded animal such as a mouse or a bird by "feeling" its body heat. Thus, the snake can hunt in the dark or down a deep hole. Although other species of snakes also have heat-sensitive organs, this sense is highly developed in the pit vipers. In this family are the rattlesnakes, the copperhead, and the cottonmouth or water moccasin. Rattlesnakes often strike from a coiled position, and although a bite is not usually fatal, it can be extremely painful and dangerous if not treated immediately.

Bush viper.

The viper family has many members, including the puff adder, the European asp, and the bush viper. Vipers are found in Asia, Africa, and Europe. The large fangs of vipers and pit vipers are hinged and kept folded up against the top of the mouth. They swing down and forward as the snake prepares to strike.

42

Asian cobra, hooded and ready to strike.

The cobras, mambas, and coral snakes are venomous snakes belonging to the elapid family. Of these, only the coral snake is found in the United States. Cobras are found in Asia and Africa and mambas only in Africa. When a cobra is alarmed, it raises its head and spreads the ribs of its neck so that the skin forms a hood. It strikes down and forward, and the bite of many species of cobras can kill a person. Several types of spitting cobras defend themselves by spraying venom into the eyes of an intruder to temporarily blind it. This gives the cobra time to escape.

The elapids are like members of the sea snake family, the hydrophiids, in that they have short fangs which are in a fixed position and firmly fastened like their other teeth. Sea snakes live in tropical waters. They have flattened tails, which they use as paddles when swimming.

43

Jamaican boa, an endangered species.

Snakes have lived on earth for millions of years. However, like other wild animals, some species of snakes are now endangered, particularly in places where farms and cities have expanded into areas in which the snakes live and in remote areas where land is being developed for recreation. The use of off-road vehicles in the desert, for instance, has upset the delicate balance of life there and threatened some desert-dwelling reptiles. Sometimes people also kill snakes for sport or because they believe them to be dangerous. Some large snakes are killed for their beautiful skins, which

are then used to make shoes, belts, and other articles.

Like all living creatures, snakes are part of the balance of nature. As natural predators of mice and rats, they play a valuable role in keeping the rodent population under control.

Snakes are a highly diverse group whose many species live in a wide variety of habitats and whose size, shape, color, and behavior vary enormously. There are so many different kinds of snakes that scientists are only beginning to learn about the daily lives of some of them.

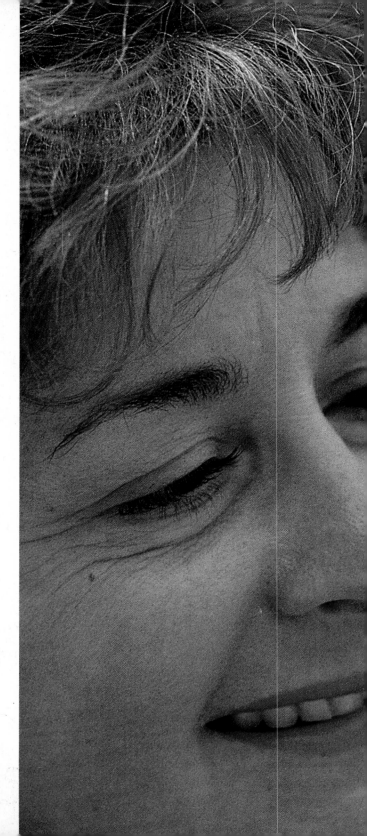

People who study snakes are called herpetologists, from the Greek word for "creeping" or "crawling," referring to the way snakes move around. You don't have to be a herpetologist to enjoy learning about snakes, though. Some people who keep snakes and other small reptiles as pets belong to clubs where they meet and share information. You can also see snakes in a zoo or try to observe them in the wild. Educational programs such as those of the Los Angeles Zoo help people to discover the unique qualities of snakes by allowing them to see animals like the rosy boa up close.

People have been fascinated by snakes for a long time. No other land animal is as long as some snakes or possesses the same combination of special senses for detecting prey. As we learn more about these long, slithering creatures, we can appreciate their special qualities and find out how useful each snake is and how well suited it is to the place in which it lives.

Index

Photographs are in **boldface.**

Baby, 3, **16–17,** 17, **28**

desert, 11, 12, 23, 44

jungle, 11, 15, 18

lizards, 10, 11, 19, 24, 27, 31, 33
Los Angeles Zoo, 3, 7, 8, **8, 9,** 11, 17, 31, 46
    staff, 7–8, **9, 16–17,** 17, 31
    visitors, 8, **8, 9**

reptiles, 7, 8, 10–11, 44
Rosy, 4, **4–5, 6–7,** 7, 29, **30,** 31, 32

snake
    babies, 17, 33, **33, 34,** 35, 37
    backbone, 18, **20–21,** 21
    body, 4, 10, 12–15, 18–19, 21–22, 29, 33, 35,
      39
    ears, 29
    eating, 11, 28, 37
    eyes, 15, 16, 27, **36,** 37, 39
    families, 39
      blind snakes, 39
      boids, 14
        boas, 8, **9,** 10, 14–16, **14, 15,** 19, 23, 39,
          44–45
        rosy boa, **1,** 4, **4–5, 6–7,** 7, **10, 11,**
          12–14, **12, 13, 22–23,** 24, 27, **30,**
          31–33, **32, 33, 36,** 46, **46–47**
        pythons, 10, 14, 16–17, **16–17, 18,** 19,
          19, 23, **26, 29, 34,** 39
      colubrids, **3,** 24, **25, 34, 38,** 39, 40

elapids, 39, 43, **43**
pipe snakes, 39
pit vipers, 39, 41
    rattlesnakes, 10, **20–21,** 23–25, **36,**
      40–41, **41**
sea snakes, 39, 43
shieldtail snakes, 39
sunbeam snake, 39
vipers, 24, **24,** 39, 42, **42**
fangs, 40, **40,** 42, 43
female, 13, 19, 32–33, **32,** 35
food, 8, 14, 15, 27, 28–29, **30,** 31–33, 35
head, 4, 12, 18, 22, 43
legs, 18–19, **19,** 39
life span, 17, 37
male, 13, 19, 32, **32,** 35
mouth, 14, 28, 29, 31, 35, 40, 42
movement, 15, 22–24, 46
predators, 16, 24, 25
reproduction, 13, 16, 32–33, 35
    egg laying, 16, 32, **34,** 35
    live bearing, 16, 32
resting, 24, 27
scales, 4, 10, **10,** 12, 23, 27, 37, 39
skin, 10, 31, **36,** 37, 43, 44
swimming, 15, 22, 43
tail, 12, 13, 18, 19, 21, 22, 25, 39
teeth, 14, 29, **29,** 31, 43
temperature, 10–11, 35
tongue, 4, 28, **28**
venom, 25, 40–41, 43
vent, 13, 19, 31, 33
wild, 11–12, 13, 14, 15, 31, 32, 39, 40, 41, 42,
    43, 44–45